This Little Tiger book belongs to:

_____

_____

_____

LITTLE
TIGER PRESS
An imprint of Magi Publications
1 The Coda Centre, 189 Munster Road,
London SW6 6AW • www.littletigerpress.com

First published
in Great Britain 2010
This edition published 2011
Text and Illustrations copyright © Catherine Rayner 2010
Catherine Rayner has asserted her right to be identified as the author
and illustrator of this work under the Copyright, Designs and Patents Act, 1988
A CIP catalogue record for this book is available from the British Library
All rights reserved • ISBN 978-1-84895-092-4 • Printed in China
LTP/1800/0208/0511
2 4 6 8 10 9 7 5 3 1

For Archie x

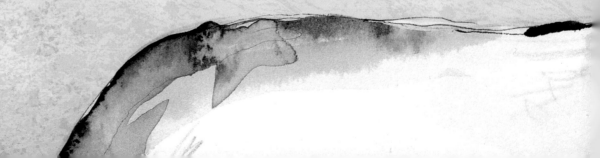

Catherine Rayner

Iris and Isaac

LITTLE TIGER PRESS
London

Iris and Isaac

were **not friends** any more.

Iris had made a snow nest but it was too
small for them both. Isaac had tried
to wriggle and nudge, and shove
his big bottom in.

Iris had wriggled and nudged, and shoved
his big bottom straight back out!
In, out, wriggle, shove,
until . . .

... they had **squashed**
the nest flat!

Iris stomped away
in a big bear huff . . .

so Isaac stomped away in a
not-quite-so-big bear huff too.

Iris was tramping grumpily across the smooth snow

when she saw a flock of Eiders soaring high in the sky.

"Look! It's the ducks!" she gasped.
But Isaac was not there to see them.

Isaac was stomping along when he
spotted two Arctic foxes playing together
on the sparkly ice.

"That looks like fun," he thought,
and sighed, and stomped off
once more.

Iris was trudging slowly
when she found a
huge echoey
ice cave.

"Oh wow! Isaac would love this!" she thought. "If only he was here."

Isaac was plodding sadly and he saw
the northern lights flicker and swirl.
"Iris adores the lights," he thought to himself.
"I wish she was here to see them too."

Then as he wandered further,

Isaac saw the most wonderful

thing of all . . .

It was Iris!

Iris and Isaac were happy once more.
They gently shuffled and nudged,
and patted and shaped,

until they had made the **perfect**
snow nest to curl up inside . . .

. . . together.

Magical books to share from Little Tiger Press!

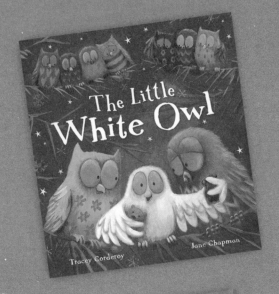

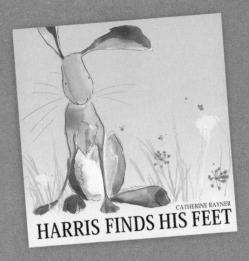

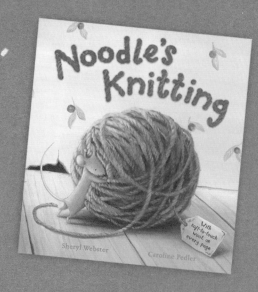

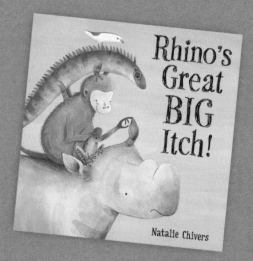

For information regarding any of the above titles
or for our catalogue, please contact us:
Little Tiger Press, 1 The Coda Centre,
189 Munster Road, London SW6 6AW
Tel: 020 7385 6333 • Fax: 020 7385 7333
E-mail: info@littletiger.co.uk • www.littletigerpress.com